The Adventures of Kip

Shelley Shultz

Tellwell Talent
www.tellwell.ca

ISBN
978-0-2288-7573-4 (Hardcover)
978-0-2288-7572-7 (Paperback)

With his fluffy tail and little feet, no wonder Kip
makes friends with everyone he meets.

He likes to walk right by my side, but when he gets tired, he gets a ride.

He makes a little bark when he sees a person or another dog go by. That tells me he wants to say "hi".

The most special time for Kip is when
he knows he is going on a trip.

Whether he travels by car or by plane, Kip is
so happy to be going and is never a pain.

He is as quiet as a mouse, as long as he's
not left behind at the house.

He doesn't mind not knowing where he is going.
He doesn't care, as long as he gets there.

Instead of walking, he starts to run, because
the life of Kip is so much fun.

When in France, he loves to dance.

He wears his best tie and enjoys watching the people go by.

When at the bakery or boulangerie, he eats a croissant (and saves a bite for me).

When he boards the train, he says, "Au revoir."
Since dogs can't talk, he raises his paw.

Kip settles in for a nap on the train, and
in six hours he will be in Spain.

The sea is as beautiful as it can be. So taking
a short swim will be perfect for him.

After a visit with the macaque monkeys at
the tip, it's time to say "chao" for Kip.

He's still not ready to go home, so he boards
the train for the city of Rome.

He'll visit fountains and mountains, a
museum and the Colosseum.

After eating oodles of noodles, it is time for some gelato.

"Always save room for some dessert" is Kip's motto.

Kip says, "Ciao" for now, as he takes a bow.

Kip loved his trip. He visited France, Spain, and the city of Rome. Now he's finally ready to go home.

After he boards the plane and takes his
seat, he waits patiently for his treat.

Kip saw so many interesting places, but home
is still one of his favorite spaces.

It feels so good to just be chill, and practicing
yoga is Kip's greatest thrill.

Shelley Shultz is a retired teacher and elementary school counselor. Her love of children, animals, travel and cultural experiences were the driving force behind her first children's book. Shelley lives in South Florida with her husband and 15-year-old Shih tzu, Kip. She and Kip enjoy their daily yoga practice, amongst other activities.

Made in the USA
Middletown, DE
15 December 2022

18690218R00020